For Ellie

Don't Put Your Finger in the Jelly, Nelly!

by Nick Sharratt

Don't put your finger
in the jelly,
Nelly!

You might
upset a
jellyphant!

Don't put your finger
in the pie,
Guy!

Don't put your finger
in the cheese,
Louise!

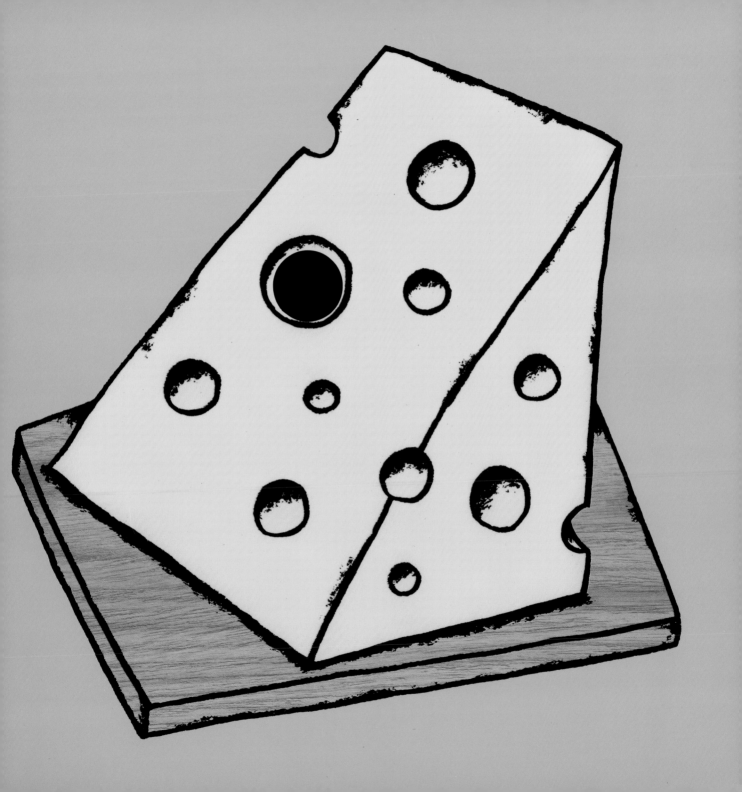

You'll get caught by an alligrater!

Don't put your finger
in the jam,
Sam!

It's clawberry flavour!

Don't put your finger
in the pasta,
Jocasta!

Don't put your finger
in the shake,
Jake!

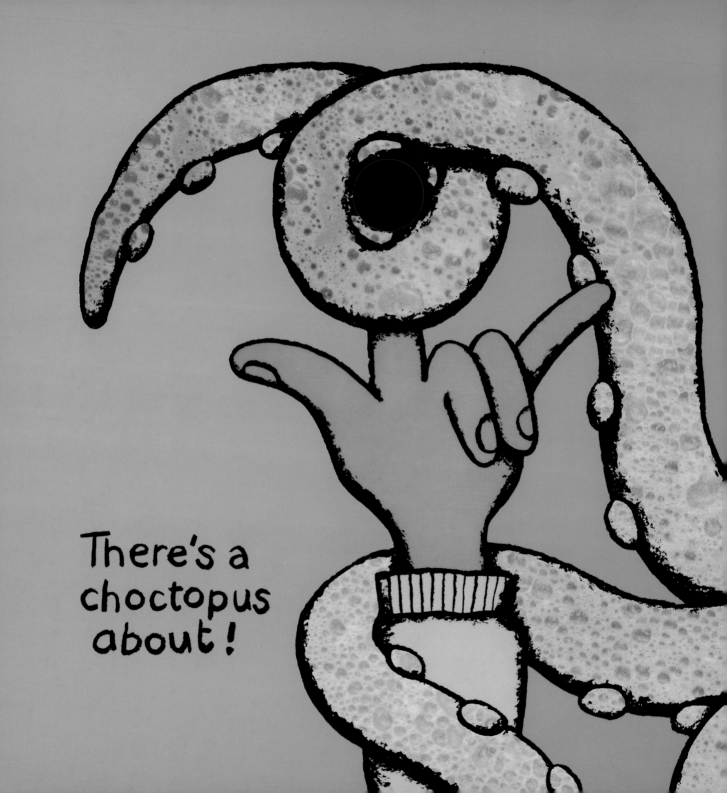

There's a
choctopus
about!

Don't put your finger
in there,
Claire!

Unless
you like
doughnuts,
that is!

Scholastic Children's Books,
Commonwealth House, 1-19 New Oxford Street,
London WC1A 1NU, UK
a division of Scholastic Ltd
London ~ New York ~ Toronto ~ Sydney ~ Auckland

First published in the UK by Scholastic Ltd, 1993
This edition published in the UK by Scholastic Ltd, 1996

Copyright © Nick Sharratt, 1993

ISBN 0 590 13664 X

Printed and bound in Hong Kong by Paramount Printing Group Ltd

10 9 8 7 6 5 4 3 2 1

The right of Nick Sharratt to be identified as the author of this work has been asserted by him in accordance
with the Copyright, Designs and Patents Act, 1988.

Photographs by Edgardo Braggio, Fotacha Ltd

A book for all dippers and pickers!
(with real holes that little fingers
can explore!)

Don't Put Your Finger in the Jelly, Nelly!
is for people who like to dip their fingers
into anything that looks tasty – though
they might be in for a bit of a shock!

Picture Hippo

ISBN 0-590-13664-X

9 780590 136648 >